EARTHQUACK!

EARTHQUACK!

By Margie Palatini

Illustrated by Barry Moser

SCHOLASTIC INC.
New York Toronto London Auckland Sydney
Mexico City New Delhi Hong Kong Buenos Aires

Little Chucky Ducky

had just finished swimming his morning laps. He dried off his bill, wiped off his two webbed feet, and was letting the water roll off his back, when suddenly . . .

He heard the ground grumble. He felt the ground rumble. And then, with a stumble, Chucky Ducky went down in a tumble!

"Oh, good golly!" quacked the duck as he got up and unruffled his feathers. "The earth is crumbling! The earth is crumbling! Why, it's a quake!" he quacked. "I have to warn my friends!"

Without a minute to waste, Chucky Ducky waddled and flapped and flapped and waddled across the meadow, where he saw Lucy Goosey.

"The earth is crumbling! The earth is crumbling! It's a quake!" quacked the duck.

The goose gave a gander. "Are you sure?" asked Lucy, not at all convinced.

"Of course I'm sure," answered Chucky Ducky. "I heard what I heard. I felt what I felt. I saw what I saw—and I saw it!"

And then, suddenly . . . right below their four webbed feet . . .

They heard the ground grumble. Then they felt the ground rumble. And before they knew it, Chucky Ducky and Lucy Goosey were taking a tumble!

"The earth is crumbling! The earth is crumbling!" honked the goose.

"I tell you, it's a quake!" quacked the duck. "We have to warn our friends!"

Without a minute to waste, Chucky Ducky and Lucy Goosey waddled and flapped and flapped and waddled up to the barnyard. And who should they meet scratching and hatching but Vickie, Nickie, and Rickie Chickie?

"The earth is crumbling! The earth is crumbling! It's a quake!" quacked the duck.

"Is this some kind of trick?" cheeped a chick.

"I heard what I heard. I felt what I felt. I saw what I saw—and I saw it!" said Chucky Ducky.

"Me too!" said Lucy Goosey.

And then, suddenly . . . right below their four webbed feet and six little chicken legs . . .

They heard the ground grumble. Then they felt the ground rumble. And before they knew it, they were all taking a tumble!

"The earth is crumbling!" cheeped the chicks.

"The earth is crumbling!" honked the goose.

"I tell you, it's a quake!" quacked the duck. "We have to warn our friends!"

Without a minute to waste, Chucky Ducky, Lucy Goosey, and Vickie, Nickie, and Rickie Chickie flapped and waddled and waddled and flapped in a troop up to the coop, where they saw Brewster Rooster.

"The earth is crumbling! The earth is crumbling! It's a quake!" quacked the duck.

"Sound the alarm!" honked the goose.

"Excuse me. But I only doodle-doo once a day," said the rooster calmly, raking a comb through his feathers. "Read my job description."

"But you just gotta crow!" cried the three little chicks.

"Yes! Yes!" said Chucky Ducky. "I heard what I heard. I felt what I felt. I saw what I saw—and I saw it!"

"Me too!" honked Lucy Goosey.

"We three!" cheeped Vickie, Nickie, and Rickie Chickie.

And then, suddenly . . . right below their four webbed feet, six little chicken legs, and two big drumsticks . . .

They heard the ground grumble. Then they felt the ground rumble. And before they knew it, they were all taking a tumble!

"The earth is crumbling!" squawked the rooster.

"The earth is crumbling!" cheeped the chicks.

"The earth is crumbling!" honked the goose.

"I tell you, it's a quake!" quacked the duck. "We have to warn our friends!"

Without a minute to waste, Brewster Rooster let out a crow.

"Cock-a-doodle-dooooooooooooooo!"

"So what's new?" asked Sue Ewe, hoofing it on over to Brewster Rooster with her lambs, Sam and Pam.

"Yes, what's the big to-do?" grumbled Nanny Goat, not pleased that all the hubbub had awakened Billy the kid from his afternoon nap.

"Yeah, you're interrupting my lunch," snorted Iggy Piggy, wiping his snout in a pout.

"The earth is crumbling! The earth is crumbling! I tell you, it's a quake!" quacked the duck.

"Oh, it can't be that baa-ad," sighed Sam, Pam, and Sue.

"It sounds nutty to me," said Merle Squirrel, going out on a limb.

"But I heard what I heard. I felt what I felt. I saw what I saw—and I saw it!" quacked the duck.

"Hogwash!" grunted the pig.

And then, suddenly . . . they all heard a grumble. They all felt a rumble. And then, one by one, they all went down with a tumble!

"Run for the hills!" snorted Iggy Piggy.

"Take to the trees!" squealed Merle Squirrel.

"The doorway! The doorway! You ninnies," nayed little Billy.

So they listened to the kid and ran to the door of the big red barn and huddled and cuddled and hoped they were safe from any more rumbling, grumbling, and most of all, crumbling.

Now several yards away, under a sticky thicket, watching all the commotion, was one very hungry weasel.

"Mmm-mmmm-mmmmm," he muttered greedily, licking his lips. "Lamb chops. Bacon. Roast goose. Chicken and squirrel stew. Yum, yum!"

The wormy weasel grinned. "My pantry is pretty paltry, but I have an idea that will get their goat and give me one big banquet buffet!"

So, without a minute to waste, the sneaky weasel climbed out from the sticky thicket, made out a menu for the month, and then cleverly disguised himself in his long white winter coat.

"The earth is crumbling! The earth is crumbling!" he shouted, running toward the barn.

"You know about the quake?" quacked the duck from the doorway.

"I heard what I heard. I felt what I felt. I saw what I saw—and I saw it!" lied the weasel.

Brewster Rooster pointed a wing and cocked his head with suspicion. "I've never seen you around here before. Who exactly are you?"

"Name's Herman Ermine," the weasel said with a sly smile. "As it happens, I'm an expert in rumbles and crumbles. In fact, I have a quakeproof hideaway not too far from here. You'll be much much safer if you come with me."

"Yes! Yes! We want to be safe!" they all said, rushing from the doorway of the big red barn and lining up behind Herman Ermine, not knowing he was really a lying, conniving, wily weasel.

So off went Chucky Ducky, Lucy Goosey, Vickie, Nickie, and Rickie Chickie, Brewster Rooster, Sue Ewe with her two lambs, Pam and Sam, Nanny Goat, Billy the kid, Merle Squirrel, and Iggy Piggy. Into the deep, dark, thickest thickets of the woods the group trooped.

After a ways and a while, the weasel stopped. He pointed. "Down here," he said with a sneer.

Vickie, Nickie, and Rickie Chickie took a peep. "But that just looks like a hole," cheeped the chicks.

"A deep, dark hole," noticed Nanny.

"And it looks like such a long way down," said Sam and Pam.

"Come now. Don't be sheepish," said the weasel, sidling up to Sue and already planning a supper of lamb stew.

He was just about to give Chucky Ducky the first shove down the hole, when suddenly . . .

There was a grumble. Then a rumble. And the ground around the weasel started to crumble!

First a trip—then a stumble—right through the thicket—out of his white winter coat.

"Uh-oh. I think I made a fumble."

"Well, what a weaselly little fellow!" crowed Brewster Rooster, waving the white winter coat. "Thank goodness we are safe!"

"But I tell you, it's still a quake!" quacked the duck as the earth grumbled, rumbled, and crumbled all around their feet.

"Yes! It's still a quake!" they all shouted. "It's a quake! It's a quake!"

"It's not a quake," said two heads suddenly poking up from the dirt.

"It's not a quake?" they all said.

"It's just us," the two answered with a wink and a blink. "Joel and Lowell Mole."

"Joel and Lowell Mole?" they all said, looking at one another.

"You mean, the earth isn't grumbling?" squawked Lucy Goosey, Brewster Rooster, and the three little chickies.

"You mean the earth isn't rumbling?" squealed Iggy Piggy and Merle Squirrel.

"You mean the earth isn't crumbling?" cried out Nanny, Billy, Pam, Sam, and Sue.

"No quake?" quacked Chucky Ducky.

"We don't know anything about grumbles, rumbles, crumbles, or quakes," mumbled the moles stumbling out from their holes.

"We're just looking for our cousin, Garret Ferret. . . . Does anybody know the way to San Jose? We think we took a wrong turn at the Lincoln Tunnel."

Wrong turn, indeed.

So they all showed Joel and Lowell which way to go.

And out of the woods and back to the barnyard went Iggy Piggy, Merle Squirrel, Nanny Goat, Billy the kid, Sue Ewe and her lambs, Sam and Pam, Brewster Rooster, Vickie, Nickie, and Rickie Chickie, Lucy Goosey, and . . . that little quack, Chucky Ducky.

Who, right from the beginning, was all wet.

*For my family's unforgettable trip
through the Lincoln Tunnel
—M. P.*

*For Ava Simone Harper, my beautiful Sixth
—B. M.*

ISBN 0-439-58746-8

Text copyright © 2002 by Margie Palatini. Illustrations copyright © 2002 by Barry Moser. All rights reserved. Published by Scholastic Inc., 557 Broadway, New York, NY 10012, by arrangement with Simon & Schuster Books for Young Readers, Simon & Schuster Children's Publishing Division. SCHOLASTIC and associated logos are trademarks and/or registered trademarks of Scholastic Inc.

12 11 10 9 8 7 6 5 4   4 5 6 7 8/0

Printed in the U.S.A.   24

First Scholastic printing, October 2003

The text for this book is set in 17-point Caslon 224 Book.

The paintings were executed in graphite and transparent watercolor on Fabriano, handmade at the Cartiere Miliani Fabriano Mills in Fabriano, Italy.